THE FOUL DRIVE

VICTORY OVER HALLUCINATION

SUMEET KUMAR

ISBN 979-888606129-1

Sumeet Kumar

Sumeet Kumar , A adult who experiences many phases of love in his life , get broked many times , stands up every time and keep moving to the next phases of the life.In reality he is a writter as well as singer (as a hobby). Very exciting and interesting fact about him is that he is author of New era i.e. he starts his journey of writing at the age when he was going to schools to get the study . His some famous works i.e. Maturity Of Love (Genre - Love),Privacy For Dream (Genre - Middle Class), Army Squad ofLove (Genre- The Seperation of Army Love), 5 Days of Love(Genre- Temporarily Love), Th e Endearment Of Love(Genre - Historical Era Of Love), Social Destruction Indo-Pak (Genre - The Story of The Love At The Time Of Division Of India And Pakistan), Middle Class Soul (Genre - The Dreams of Middle Class), The Accursed Kanatpur (Genre -The Horrific Story Of A Village), Wrong Number (Genre -The Suspenseful Physco Killer Story), The Secrecy OfDeadly Midnight (Genre - The Suspense About a Crime),Fragile Religious Of Death (Genre- The Death Of A TrustfulPerson), Nature Vs Science (Genre - The Future Battle Between Nature And Science In A Horrific Way), Generic Man (Genre - The Dream of I.I.T), The Unconsious 12 Hours(Genre - The Illusion At Stage Of Comma), The StrangeBurden (Genre - The Burden Of Love) , Her Existence (Genre- The Female Pain In The Society) , Jockstrap Prize (Genre -The True Story Of A National Athlete) , H Man [Hindi] (Genre - Superhero Tragic Story), H Man [English] (Genre - Superhero Tragic Story) , Maturity Of Love [Englsih] (Genre - Love) and many more are available on various geners on the offcial platform of Amazon, Flipkart and Notionpress. You can buy them from there.

Contents

Acknowledgements   *vii*

1. Deprived With Identity   1

2. The Illusion Of Time   7

3. Heaven And Hell Is Near In Business   13

Acknowledgements

Aman Kumar

Special Thanks to **Aman Kumar** who worked so hard in the preparation of this book. He has continually put with my passive voice, omission of words, and late night calls. You have be en wonderful. Thanks to him for his precious time in reviewing proposals , individual chapters and early drafts, along with his suggestions on the applicability of the material to the world.

I
Deprived With Identity

There is a lot to write today, the silence of the male question has made me so hurt myself that I can not understand these things, it is now over to understand that the love of anyone in the world is not common. Tell me that it is not easy to understand it, this proverb is famous in the handwriting of every pen that love begins when the walls of silence make their troubles till the extent that even their shadow is the party to see many dreams of trouble. Why do I feel guilty when I have started this thing only in the beginning How, Forget the moments that I have spent with him, He said very easily that I may not be able to handle my own feet. How I said and Leave her now that she is not going to come back and there is no need to bear the trouble, there is no tradition left in her memories, nor is there any tradition of being bereft in herself. She has progressed a lot in her life, why don't you move forward? People do a lot in love, they also suffer a lot and They also fight with the lights of society. Understand that only the nature, people also give birth in love, that too without any donation, it is common to leave someone, that too for a male witness who has only made appearances, he feet in front of that full gathering, has he not done anything wrong? Nor was it wrong, it was in the wrong spirit, which I did not care about, which I didn't care about The trust of one's own silence becomes its own I am always saying that someone's love for love is bad, there is a question that why you have to lose your love in his love that you will never love yourself again. I may not be aware enough think about him all the time remember his every habit. Requesting to keep time close to him is not a bad habit, our nature is our fault and as long as we try to understand it, those laughing moments of our life become so far away from us that we do not have any information about the time which breaks. It is a narration that always reminds us that we feel man's pain, the feet never ask him to remove himself from himself and how to do it: undefined memories of unfaithful male unfaithfulness which is included in it. With time, our destiny to live has been connected to us, neither can we say to die nor try to live because no one is with us at the time, so even the words of yard are useless without any reason. There is no peace and a new girl's life has been saved because the limit of pain has always been the same for one in love. Due to some condition or the other, it breaks inside itself, neither the question has arisen at the right time, nor does that answer come at the right time. When a witness tries to know himself, it clearly means that He has forgotten himself, has suffocated his own happiness, he too has come under someone else's words, before that the light of society did not allow him to live, now his friends have also prepared a curse for him whose arrest Inside he himself is wishing for death It is that even the donation of time seems small to us. If the love is incomplete, then people live their whole life by remembering each other. Even your companions cannot take it without him, love is that poison whose love is very different and very dangerous than the thinking of a common man without his love, everyone's life needs a new way. It is the place where we forget our relationships and leave their arms and are in search of someone else's heart, the thought of a human being has passed away long ago that everyone in life will not talk about the last journey with you, this pain of pain There is no cost and there is no such education in the market filled with the love of a witness, why am I writing these bottles and I am justifying that I have been guilty of my words, I do not have any such desire, nor can I give it to myself. I am worthy of the happiness of the share, nor do I ask for the reason for my sorrow without any reason, even if I have found the love of pain, if I change my thinking in the feet because of any one witness, then I will be happy, I will forget the time, that too full gathering where there will be some people who care about me, I don't even talk about anything because my anger is with me and I never say to fall in his eyes because I know if I am hurt He will be in a lot of trouble and I will never give trouble to my rhetoric, saying that every thing in the world has been written as a gift to get feet, Despite being famous in love, how the feet of ruin come: why people have not written about it, they give the gift of getting those two because our love is compelled to say that to anyone who got his eyes from the eyes of his family. To go to society, waste is not too far away from you, that enough is waiting for your fate in waiting for you The day the first wind of love is felt, some days the silence becomes a saying and the kind of saying is worse than intoxication because even after its descent, we remain slaves to it somewhere, it is that innocent sweetheart who will never be far away from us. Tries and says not to come near, it is we ourselves who give it the place of our gathering, where once our happiness had made the Taj Mahal, that too our friends. People suddenly feel weak and never party to break them. The conspiracy is such that they are never able to know themselves at some time and how can they even say that they are aware, they care about themselves. tears gives up his own habit and uncountable happiness also donates a small amount of happiness in someone else's bag and at the same time his reason is also very bad because he says that breaking legs is the memory of yard and he Even friends, we are never able to hurt ourselves, we try to share our man's pain with everyone, yet the price of man's pain never works. Why not alived towards someone else, yet that reason is never changed, enough remains alive in his mind that no matter how much we tell him, the legs cannot separate themselves at the moment. Did you know ? some pronounciation which i call everyone as kehna even i ask to explain myself like an ilm, when a bridge of love starts then our innocence and our ages then time become very close to them too There is no news that both of them can never become friends of each other, even after cahh because their thinking is different, their weights are different and even their habits are different from each other, then even when there is love, we both love us. Recommends a very close lane, he himself does not love anyone else You must be thinking that why I am saying both the conversation means a one sided against them and also with them on the other sided, this is the only thing that is true when we meet some aishe witness and seeing him for the first time, our future is with him. When we do imagine to spend, it starts with those two paths, which neither he had ever seen his soul, nor had any health about him. I have heard that because when the time seems to be short, some people explain their pain, no one does it completely because they never say to go close to the gathering, they also see the time of their pain in front of their eyes and ask them When a witness moves forward in his life by fighting, he never asks to go to the old gathering again, nor does he ask to repeat his friends with any other witness, because the fear he has seen in his eyes is also that of losing someone. Then he does not ask to see, people say that the first love is not forgotten, hey it is right foot, why do they forget those relationships in someone else's love, who never left their side, every recommendation of pain when he got it, every time he got it were close with him then why did he forget those relationships I have said this for the first time that the price of pain is a lot of work, if in the world he is also in love, then it becomes very easy to get whatever I lost. I can't get my soul again. I will never change my relationship and whatever I have, I will never give them any trouble because when someone was broken in love, neither he is alone nor he gets the walls of pain in a hot wedding, but his time with him. There are also disciples who travel through human pain, neither trying to repeat the human pain nor trying to ask themselves to be small in someone else's love, because in the world of love, there is a desire for pain that he should be a good friend.

"Not only the time is involved but my whole life is involved in it
In the situation when i become alone,
I think who becomes my well wishers , not beome
a destroyer of my world
neither i have any wishes of anyone
nor wishes of anoyone's support
Only she should return my happiness
those who becomes the killer of my dreams."

II

The Illusion Of Time

All the time, if only one thing keeps in mind, then it
does not mean that we are very close to him, it is very close
to us, in the same way, I am doing things for those people

who think that life can meet many better people than us. The more unfulfilled dreams we have, the better life is, the day those dreams become real Does man try to fulfill the dream, neither those dreams ever come true nor his life No, but a boy can also be in his place because when both the sexes were created in the world, they never thought that a word of infidelity will be made, that too can understand for the human race, a witness can be forced He can break, it can torment him from inside at the time of his condition that he can never stand back on his feet. Where is the beginning of this? In reality, does anyone have any news, undefined people live their whole lives, then they stand up to death, like girls in a golgape shop, these days, keeping a long limit, stays tight. Have asked the meaning of my life what she tells us undefined May be my reality, feet may not be the truth at all, even though my age is work blessed and God had written with the help of someone else, that too by making my fortune, many such moments come in our life where we consider ourselves to be a feast, we comfort ourselves all the time that this life is not meant for everyone like you. Waqt Bash conspires to ask himself small, we try to kill ourselves gracefully by giving us time and a enemy. If everything is easily found in life, then only the rules of God will change, that too against hard work, someone had said that "True love is never forgotten, it is just like life insurance after life and With life .

Quote; Without the feet, no one knew that we take our whole life, the reason for our happiness and the reason for our sorrow, in the end, our life is done in such a way that life is also incomplete by becoming a sister-in-law It seems that I do not want to make a garland of words, I have to get the education of justice from God, till today, I never feel lucky to reject anyone, so let me take you in a journey where the reason for happiness is found, I have received foot bail for the future. My feet as sorrow It was a lovely child, its age was said to die if we don't fall in love with Nandlala, then I am undefined Where do these people come from, taking such kind of sympathy, who tells them how to explain these things to them, they have no say of such sympathy? Nor do they ever need to speak these words, this party is happening to all of you in the name of our name. About us, we refer only to the pure Brahman family, the feet are very distant from the path of worship. I have hugged and don't care about their thinking and why should we care about the above, what they gave me till today, that too without parents, if you tell this incomplete story, then my reality may never come in front of you all. I try to complete the story first, that means our birth chart when I was born That's when my parents separated me from themselves, I don't know the reason why when Pandit ji told me these conversation, then in real time only one voice came out that why did they do this undefined Well conversation I am just joking, because the life which was given to me by the above is also a joke, neither the glory of the parents on the head nor the feet of brothers and sisters in their hands, they did it to me Except because I do not have any lessons from them because when a person's compulsion comes close to him, he first remembers his own relationships and also tries to forget and these things are in our destiny long ago. We had kept our steps in the world Just like sugar candy, well after this, when my real mother left my father, then our life came in our life.Never did we ever let us play their shortcomings and I had never seen my real parents when I opened my eyes, because when I opened my eyes, she also met at the feet of Mother Yasodha, who gave us her love with great love. In love of a mother arms, her love was clearly visible in her eyes for her son and on the other hand, my father, Vasudev Pandit, who was really my world, never returned his love to her, hard because it was that nectar. It is the one who opens many doors of love as soon as it is removed from the neck, then what was it when Mother Yashodha saw me on the banks of the Ganges Mian, then she hugged us and hid the enough in the shadow of her love because she did not tell us that time I don't know what my mother Yasodha saw in me, whenever I ask her what is special about me, she always says enough and beats that you are different, Krishna, you are not a common man. It's childhood, these conversation never used to come in the society, I never made friends in my whole life, neither did I ever come to them. The shadow never went away because father was a teacher by profession and mother Yashodha was the founder of Orphan School, where like me, there are many others like me and like me, I feel that the feet are not really special, so my studies are also father.

Being close to me, neither he would ever separate me from himself, nor mother would ever let me go out of city, by the way, let me tell the name of my sehar, both I and my mother Yashodha were of the same sehar, that means my feet from Banaras dad belonged to Nagpur, both father and mother had run away and married because both of them did not belong to the same caste, so the wheezy hives of the society came against their love like a wall from time to time, so dad thought that a It is better to start a new fight that we both run away and get married, then what if the love is true, then even a person's thinking can never rock them by meeting them and it was my mother and father that both of them were from childhood. He was a fan of Superman, then what was the matter when dad held his mother's hand and came straight to Nagpur, so let me tell you that dad has no family. My mother's family had refused to make her their jamai, in addition to this, every love story is a true story, which you must have known better that the boy has no caste, nor does he have any religion, so we give our daughter How to hand it to him After listening and thinking about all this, my mother and father decided that we should run away and get married and everyone will know that if love is two-sided and that too true, then they meet each other. then they can't even rock the upper limit and ability of a common man, what was the wish of a common man in front of everyone. Feet say that if the gathering of happiness is taking you all around as a slave in your courtyard, then there are many such secrets behind it that will take you to the gathering of sorrowless sorrow, don't try to say conversation. I am doing it and there is no narration how to do them in my feet. And what was the news to him that my presence would be made a sheet of sorrow in the gathering of his happiness, so my regret started when he again went to Banaras, when the mother went to her maternal home, she was no one next. My father asked from the side that these people who used to live earlier, where did they go, no one answered right Because she also had a world of her own, which was her parents and brothers and sisters, and due to not meeting them, she was very silent in herself and these baton dad knew very well, that's why she told her mother that let's have visit of mother Ganga. After all, when mother and father went to Maa's Ganga arms with their silence, then they saw me, near whom many people were already gathered, neither did anyone lift me in finery nor did anyone When someone tried to silence me, in reality I was made the spectacle of the activities of the society at the time, due to which they were getting happiness, after all, when When father and mother saw the new man crowd, they immediately came and gave him feet like the rest, when both of their eyes rolled me, they probably felt the pain at the time and I also gave my name to my mother's eyes. I had seen what it was then, mother immediately came out of my baby and hugged me on her chest and made me sleep in the shadow of her love, by making me cry every single moment of my life, at the feet of Mother Gange for life, handed over to.

"Wrote in the bailout, too,
so what should I write about that love?
There is no one who has been able to compare
that mother in the world.
When you were angry with me
I can't stand up in this world.
In pain i becomes a homeless being which
always want a home
Her lap were spread, come my son was called
by my mom.

Your glory that God knows and I have passed the
scriptures too
no one is better than you , no one is perfect than
you , For now I become a saint too"

III

Heaven and Hell Is Near In Business

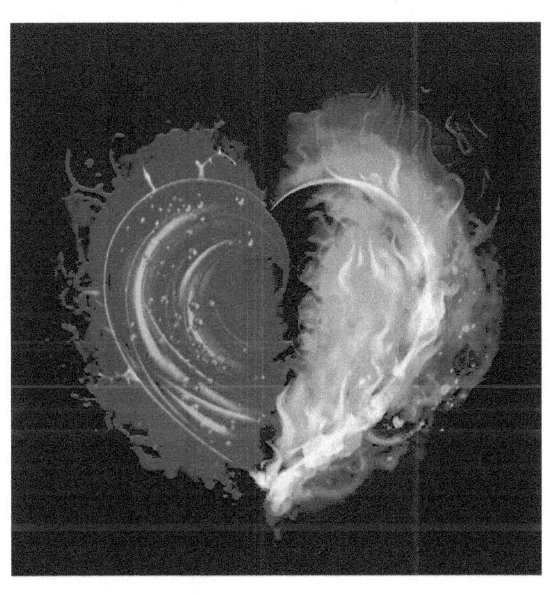

Some relationships are not for blood, feet do more than their duty to be themselves, if something in life has become away from you, it does not mean that its paths have also been closed for you for a whole life. It is hard to tell someone, God's luck also becomes silent for some time and tries very hard to bring the witness closer to his destination, if he says, then undefined Make your world such that even if someone says to you If he becomes ill for some time, then his bail should never come in front of you in silence because that witness has saved your life. It is that if someone speaks two sweet words to us, we become slaves to his baatis and if he speaks any two words, then we wash our feet after his departure, then why don't we do this after the unbearable love undefined When a witness loses himself in love, then that person comes at the time by preparing the slave of his anger and he needs to know about it. Doesn't live up to the news what he has lost? Blood relations also become like water when the smell of love comes in the gathering, we don't even say to explain at the time what is right and what is wrong for us undefined Well I know that I am sorry for taking the story of pain anywhere, I am sorry for that, so let's see how my life was ahead of him, that too in the same city of which I was very unaware, neither it was my birthplace nor that The living and specialty of me is that I have no one of my own except mother Yashodha and Papa in the gathering. I was very lucky at the time, because on one side my real parents were the ones who gave birth to mother Ganga. And on the other hand, Mother Yashodha's unknown right Gaur, who made Maa Gange then my relatioship own by China It is said that the wind of luck blows first when the tradition of birth is very distant from our feet, after all, when the mother hugged me then that time her husband means my father didn't even say anything enough all those books were left that who left it has anyone seen it undefined they asked almost everyone at that time whatever time they were present feet someone Didn't answer all then enough was saying that why don't you leave it in an orphanage, if you guys are so concerned then undefined good times, I don't know enough, remember mother Yashodha's batis who heard from such a witness who He also had the world and my mother also told him so much at the time that if anyone thinks that he is an orphan, then leave from me and if anyone has said this again in front of my Krishna, then his death is at my hands. This will be my son, my Nandlala, what was my mother Yashodha's Kanha then after listening to the words of the mother, neither the light of the society came to the fore nor did her thoughts, after all, the mother thought that now we should teach it further. Gone and will make a big man, where the thinking of the society and its lights will never be able to reach it, I am surprised that why did the witness did not ask any question? We do not have sons undefined and if we have children then why should we have him undefined because we should give him the status of first child undefined it is neither our blood nor our upbringing undefined and if his parents were accidentally exposed yesterday Then how will you take care of them? It was because the idol of human being was my mother Yashodha, I probably did not deserve to become his Kanha because till today I have not given him any happiness, if there is any bigger thing than human being, then my mother was only Yashodha at that time. I am requesting not to write to mine, because whatever my life is ahead of it, it is neither worth telling nor worth expressing, yet I will never leave the gift of getting them, whose way is still to my relationship. Are connected with those roads whose same face always turns into pain. It comes to the fore. After all, when mother and father brought me to Nagpur, they also faced many arguments in the beginning, in the society, many things about me, who's blood, who is undefined, did not bring them by stealing from somewhere. undefined There were many other things which I neither say to repeat nor express because these are the idiots of the society and the thoughts that take them very far away from every humanity, then for many years they have to face the same things. In the end, even after doing his thinking, he got a box in a grave like his conversation, whose walls neither contained the same noise as before, nor could he ever forget those batis in slander, nor the circumstances which My mother Yashodha and my father had suffered, they were not even at fault, yet why did society tell them such things undefined why they should face those walls which were related to my existence undefined Was in the wrong spirit and my real mother Father was then why did they both get such punishment undefined Mother Yashodha always used to say that if you do something good in the world. If yes, then that truth will take you forward. And the sins that became my destiny, used to remind me of a silence at all times in those moments of childhood, now that world was also very difficult for me, that too because of my mother and father, they not only nurtured me and grew up, but also her Instead, he gave me his name, his home and more than that, the respect that society had never given me and I can never forget the immense love that I found in his shadow every single day. I changed my life for everyone. My destiny had changed completely now. Mother used to tell me to become a big person as she thought. I know this much that my mother and my father were very happy on each day and the tears that I saw in their eyes were not ordinary tears but their family. There was a teacher who was associated with every single script of my fate, in which neither did he tell them to lose their time nor did they ever tell them to be free, in which enough used to keep them with him at all times by holding them in his arms. (Now all You must also be thinking that this story has not progressed a little sooner because now it was full of sorrows, and the bitter feelings have also come, saying this is not a film. I am a hero, this toh bash is the request of life and time, Gujar Singh is making my moments to run away with time Don't wait till now and don't leave in front of you and if all of you were thinking about films, then let me tell you one thing that our life is also not work from any film because in this also the parameters of sorrow and happiness are same. As it happens. My success had also become a training for such a journey in our gathering, which is called a deception in our gathering, it is a walk on a path that wishes you a very long success. He will walk with a foot from where you will never ask him to return, nor will your nature allow you to accept it, since childhood, it was a dream to become a business mind because even his ruin would have many benefits, his wealth would never die and Nor did his companions ever follow him, I was born in the thinking of my middle class family, my feet love was completely different from my parents. The one who was a very honest teacher of the Boards school, I knew long ago that he was not a common school because he also used to study the sons of ministers and some senior officers, whose intellect was a work, in the matter of wealth, he Everyone was a father and I wanted this thing because at the time of 12th it was board exams and the studies of those rich were also not very good, so I started balak and white combination at the time, which was also a Chanakya policy for me. It was known that if they do not get those questions, then they will never be able to pass in the board exams, so agree. Played a game at a young time, that too to take myself towards such a height, which my mother thought long ago, she did not say in her feet that she would never know the truth that my success is also related to someone's unfailing success, either its comes from the bad work , this difference does not matter because society only sees your farg, not your thinking and the witness who sees your thinking recommends to stay very far away from the glory of the witness because he himself can achieve his fate at the grave foot. For 12th board question was enough time to get out, which is also called layacade in common words because those question was none other than Vasudev Pandit who was my father in blood, looking after him, his question was made and then he became Feet used to go straight to the exam center, feet were made where dad would never take me, the reason for this is my feet, maybe they did not say that if there is a stain on them tomorrow, then because of that, I don't know. His thinking was always the path of truth, his feet were always visible, feet were completely different from mine. It was not that he ever allowed me to lack anything, he used to ask me to stand on my own feet and to fulfill my mother's dream, why mother never asked me for anything except one thing that you are a better person. And will become a big person whose example the whole world will give, so I started playing Tigram at the time, dad used to think that I do not know that place. Feet used to tell everything about my mother, that's why I had asked my mother about the place long ago, then when there was a day left in the board exams, I had got the news that her questions should also be complete now. They have been prepared, they cannot lay down their hard copy in the leg, nor could they waste their hard copy, because if the man had done anything at the time, he would have come to know about the surgery bags, it is clearly written in the books of science that the brain of a human being If the capacity is 2400bp, then it does not use it properly then it says undefined I knew if I had something. Even if I do, only Vasudev Pandit will have to suffer their consequences, meaning I never let this happen to my father and never said and I was unaware of one more thing at the time that those who have given me so much love and sometimes some thing Never let there be a shortage of him, he is my real parents, not even if I had known this thing, I would never have acted like this at the time, I could never have bothered them, because they love me more than my real parents. I used to love them because of their respect and because of my success, I was looking for a time where I can do both these things, first success and second respect undefined.

> **"They say If there is no respect in business,
> then there is no value for any evil that comes
> from it."**

That's why at this time I had to keep the respect of my father safe and also make my first step of success, so I was looking for the time when the question papers were ready and loaded in the truck because it was my love and my father's. Also worked that if the questions are once loaded in the male truck, then their entire responsibility will be over and after that whatever happens with them will be the board federation responsible then what was it like as soon as they put the questions in the paper truck When I was going to go, I had come out with a hard copy of different sets long ago, when did this bailout become possible and how? For. Today, I am going to tell you all with great leisure that if the thinking is small, then sometimes put a mat in them and if it is a big thing, then sometimes go to the mat because it never walks one way towards Fateh but every Time goes on two-way, I know that these lamps are not coming to anyone in the society right now, so I will tell you a complete charity for this then what ? Like my father, many people of the board federation were present every day, I can't do anything even by thinking about the time, the feet say that the fun of playing the game is as much as it is dangerous and for me it is at the right time. Where he can start his game quote" tigram" quot, If the questions were layed then at that time the culprit would have been no one else but only my father, I mean Vasudev would have been a pandit only. In order to move forward one has to fall down hard, drop the feet only those who are capable of him and at that time only one person was capable for all, who was his watchman, dad had told that his thinking is very dirty. And we can't even say anything to him because the board was the watchman of the head of the federations, first if we even try to say something, then he starts threatening us that by laying down the question himself, he will blame the other leg if he gets any When she said something, she was also a teacher, she used to treat them very rudely, that's why I had thought that now is the right time to shoot one arrow or two, neither will Lanka be that city nor Ravana maybe Something happened that day before the board's exam, when he was full of clap after drinking his watchman, then I secretly did the entry death and whatever

The questions were I mean hard copy of all of them all the subjects were taken out at the same time before anyone would suspect that this has caused someone to cheer with the questions on the boards, I went straight and put them in the cabin of the watchman's cabin. Where he had slept comfortably for a long time, then after doing all this he got sick and happy time I made a fake Eid and on happy Eid I sent a message to every child of the school that if the final exams are done Qestion wants to then come on the time behind the Tuli Public School's Peach Gully Foot Profession You will get all the questtions I knew they would not trust my feet so soon that's why I had already sent them the samples then did I just put the grains on my feet Do you know that so many five will go to the floor in my move, in a short time it will be 9:00 in the night, many students who were in the same school at the right time, the feet came in front of their eyes, then maybe they I used to go to identity so I thought that going in front of them will not be right now. As for the questions, I already put them in the letter box behind the school long ago and also gave a message with them that their profession is to give all the pulses in this box, they say that they don't do anything for the loyalty of the rich. It is not good because their thinking can change at any time, I knew this thing about anyone that someone or the other would definitely try to become James Bond's oil in their group, so I also wrote that if someone For someone to be clever, I will send all your exploits which are imprisoned in speech to your parents, but it was just a rumour, I did not even do such a thing, after that everyone did what I said, they said in the letter box. He picked up the questions and without seeing anything, he went deaf from the school gate in a while, I waited for a while then I went to the letter box and all the professions he was beyond I picked them up and went straight to my house in the foot Can't take those money home with you at some time because if by mistake those money is lost to Mother Yashodha If I had seen this father, then I used to ask all the questions in my childhood, probably my parents also asked me that question and I do not say that their upbringing feet should raise any question, so I put those money in a thread on a happy day. When the news came the next morning that the question was already laid out, there was an air of silence and fear everywhere, I had said a while ago that I only shot the arrow at the same time, and then I shot it at the same time. There will be two questions before being laid, I had already sent a message board to the head of the federation that who has got the questions laid down, then what was it that as soon as it happened in the morning, my success was also with me and my fate was also with me. that he had already become in famous i mean the w watchman then who next ? He was about to eat the jail air in the morning and when this reality came to the fore and all the questions were received from his cabin, then the charitable dream that had become my dream had turned into reality for a while, at last, what happened as I thought He got the dungeon and I was very happy with victory prison undefined.

"

"Try to change the time if time changes you (2),
Do sacrifice if someone sacrifices for you (2),
In Business , Profit increases when you don't
Choose the Profit but the Profit Choosen You."
"

He says that only one can punish someone for a crime that has made him, we human race can never belong to each other, nor can we enslave each other, nor have we made ourselves, every thought of the world It is made by the imagination of the upper one, saying that it is good, this is the enough difference of evil In reality, every single thought of it and it is alive itself if we do something wrong, it punishes us likewise, but at the same time someone else commits the crime, the thought of a person becomes the word of his destruction. It is only in time, that's why sometimes we try to understand the stand better and others as weak because many people have changed the attitude of human society long ago. That the enmity increases with us as much as I get happiness, then my feet were happy in the form of a deceit, my feet were always giving me this regret. Even if my parents came to know about this by mistake, then what would happen undefined Will I be able to see them in a few days, will I be able to tell them the reality, these dreams undefined What I have seen in my mother's eyes undefined Trying to forget I was doing this thing in my feet, this thing was bothering me all the time, that's why I did another trick at the time, I opened a company from the profession I had earned, it was a different type of company import and export. Emotions used to be and export their condition? This story is not over yet my autobiography is not over yet, why is it now toh enough start, I have also earned and wasted my money, which was about to come before me after becoming my love, in the same way his identity then it will be important for those who connected with my story will said ,then My wastage was none other than Vasundhara Valmiki's foot, who is this undefined suddenly who has knocked in my life, whose only one step party I took it in my destruction? You are also going to get up very soon. Everyone will have to count because at the moment my reality is also something like this means my condition is undefined.

"Someone says,
"Winning is not born with the body""

9 798886 061291